If I Had A Dog

Story and pictures by
LILIAN OBLIGADO

A GOLDEN BOOK • NEW YORK
Western Publishing Company, Inc., Racine, Wisconsin 53404

ISBN 0-307-03036-9/ISBN 0-307-60230-3 (lib. bdg.)   E F G H I J

If I had a dog, at first he would be a tiny puppy.
He would be all soft and warm, but his nose would be cold.
He would need lots of love and care.

He would need a collar and a leash and a bone to chew.
He would need a dish for his food and a bowl
of cool fresh water.

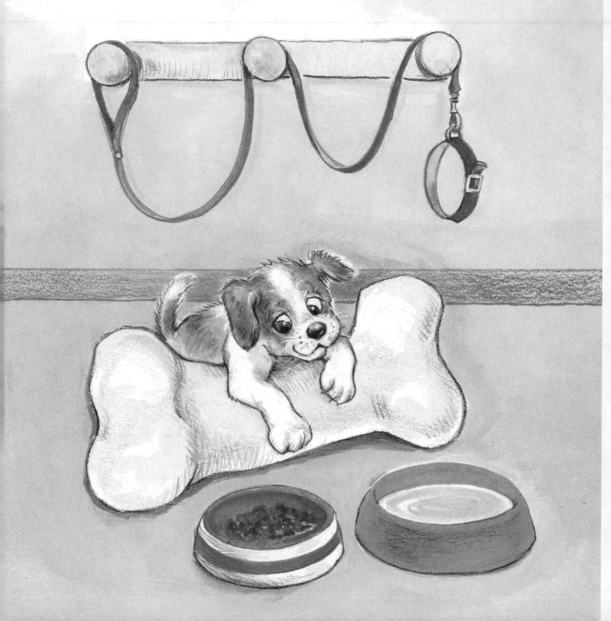

And he would need a bed of his own.

My dog would never howl all night...

or chew up shoes...

or make puddles...

or dig holes in the garden.

He wouldn't chase cats...

or leave muddy paw prints on the rug...

or eat frogs.

He would love having a bath.

Afterward, he wouldn't shake himself dry
and get me all wet.

He would be a real watchdog
and keep robbers away.

If he slept in my room I wouldn't be afraid of monsters.

He would wait for me after school.

If some bigger kids wanted to fight, he would growl at them and scare them away.

If he got hurt I would fix him up.

And if I got sick he would keep me company.

He would be helpful around the house.
He would bring Mom and Dad the newspaper every morning...
and he would help me set the table.

Maybe he would even help mow the lawn!

He would be strong enough
to give my little sister a ride.

Maybe he would give me a ride, too!

If my best friend's kitten were in trouble, he would defend her.

He would be very brave, my dog.

If we went to the beach and saw someone drowning,
my dog would risk his life to save him.

He would probably get a medal for courage.

He would be the smartest, strongest, bravest dog in the whole world.

He would love everyone, but he would love me most of all—because he would be my dog.